Zoe
the Skating
Fairy

For Aphra O'Brien

Special thanks to
Sue Mongredien

ISBN 978-0-545-20254-1

12 11 10 9 8 7 6 5 4 3   10 11 12 13 14 15/0

Printed in the U.S.A.   40

First Scholastic Printing, April 2010

Zoe
the Skating
Fairy

by Daisy Meadows

SCHOLASTIC INC.

New York   Toronto   London   Auckland
Sydney   Mexico City   New Delhi   Hong Kong

The Fairyland Palace

Fairyl

Parking Lot

Buses

Cooke Soccer Stadium

Riding Stables

Basketball Courts

Tippington Town

Soccer Fields

REC CENTER

Swimming Pool

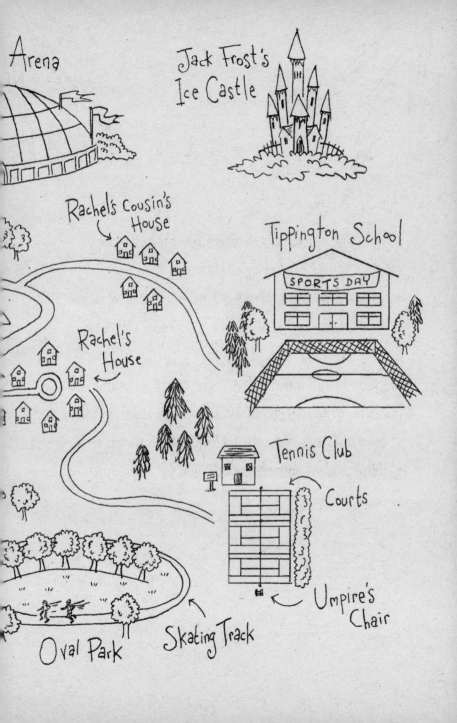

Arena

Jack Frost's Ice Castle

Rachel's Cousin's House

Tippington School

SPORTS DAY

Rachel's House

Tennis Club

Courts

Umpire's Chair

Oval Park

Skating Track

The Fairyland Olympics are about to start,
And my crafty goblins will take part.
We'll win this year, for I have a cunning plan.
I'll send my goblins to compete in Fairyland.

The magic objects that make sports safe and fun
Will be stolen by my goblins, to keep until we've won.
Sports Fairies, prepare to lose and to watch us win.
Goblins, follow my commands, and let the games begin!

Contents

Skating Struggles

Rachel Walker held on tightly to the railing as she stood up on her in-line skates. "Whoa-a-a!" She laughed, as her feet rolled in different directions. "How are you doing, Kirsty?"

Kirsty Tate, Rachel's best friend, was still sitting on the grass, tying the laces on her skates. She fastened the top straps, then smiled up at Rachel. Kirsty was staying with Rachel's family for a week during the spring vacation. Today, the girls had come to Oval Park, which was near the Walkers' house.

"All right . . . I think," Kirsty replied, clutching Rachel's hand and standing up. Then she grinned. "We must be crazy to be skating today after everything that's happened with the Sports Fairies," she said, wobbling on her wheels.

"At least we'll be nice and safe," Rachel reminded her, tapping on Kirsty's helmet. "And this is such a good place to skate, I'm sure we'll still have fun."

The girls really were being safe— with helmets, knee pads, and elbow pads, just in case one of them fell down. And Rachel was right! The park was perfect for skating, with a wide, smooth path that circled the grassy meadow. Lots of skaters and skateboarders were practicing their tricks and skills. It was a warm sunny day, with a fresh breeze rustling through the leaves in the trees, making the yellow daffodils sway back and forth.

Unfortunately, the skaters and skateboarders seemed to be getting lots of bumps and bruises today. Kirsty and Rachel watched as a boy on a skateboard

mistimed a jump and fell off his board
onto the grass nearby. He wasn't hurt
but he looked very
confused. "Why
can't I do that
jump today?" the
girls heard him
mutter to himself.

The girls
exchanged
glances. They
knew why he
was struggling with
the jump. It was because Zoe the
Skating Fairy's magic lace was missing.
That meant skaters and skateboarders
everywhere were having trouble!

Nobody else knew it—not even their
parents—but Rachel and Kirsty had

a wonderful secret. They were friends
with the fairies, and had helped them
many times! This time, they had been
called to Fairyland by King Oberon
and Queen Titania. The king and
queen had asked them to help the
Sports Fairies find their magic objects.
When the magic objects were where
they belonged—either with their fairy
keepers, or in their lockers—they
ensured that sports were fun and safe
for everyone in the human world and in
Fairyland. But when the objects weren't
where they were supposed to be, their
magic only worked on those who were
very close to the object itself.

The Fairyland Olympics were less than
a week away, and Jack Frost was set on
winning the prize—a golden cup full of

fairy luck. That was why he'd ordered his goblins to steal the magic objects from the Sports Fairies' lockers. He wanted his goblin team to win all the events, and get the prize.

Whenever the Sports Fairies did not have their special objects, things went terribly wrong with sports all over the world. Kirsty and Rachel had already helped find Helena the Horse-riding Fairy's magic riding helmet and Stacey the Soccer Fairy's magic soccer ball. But there were still five magic objects missing!

"I hope we find Zoe's magic lace soon," Rachel said, as she stepped shakily onto the path and glided forward. "I don't feel very confident on my skates today."

Kirsty nodded. "I don't, either," she replied. "But remember what Queen

Titania always says: We shouldn't go looking for fairy magic. It will find us!"

The girls set off along the path, leaning forward and swinging their arms to help them skate faster. It was hard work, though, and they kept losing their balance.

"I usually skate much better than this." Kirsty sighed as she wobbled around a corner.

Whoosh! Just then, four young skaters, wearing identical tracksuits and in-line skates, zipped past the girls at an amazing speed. Rachel and Kirsty almost fell over in surprise.

Rachel stared at them. "Well, it doesn't look like they are having any trouble," she remarked.

The girls watched the group, who were now skating in a diamond formation. They looked like young boys. But then, as the one in the front turned to say something to the one at the back, Kirsty noticed that he had a greenish tint to his skin.

"They're goblins!" Kirsty gasped.

Rachel nodded. "Yes," she said, "and since they're all skating so well, I bet they've got Zoe's magic lace with them!"

An Unexpected Shower

"After them!" cried Kirsty. She and Rachel did their best to skate faster, but it was no use. The girls were just too slow and shaky. They could tell that there was no way they were going to catch up with the speedy goblins.

"What should we do?" Rachel asked. "The goblins are already way ahead of us."

"And, look, the path goes through the woods at the next bend," Kirsty pointed out. "They'll be out of sight soon."

The girls rolled to a stop by a tree, both feeling hopeless. They watched as the goblins shot under the trees.

"Maybe we should take off our skates and run," Rachel suggested. "Then we'd be faster."

"We still wouldn't be as fast as the goblins," Kirsty replied. "They're flying!"

She sighed. "If only we had fairy wings and could *really* fly!" she added. "Then we'd be able to catch up with them."

Just then, the girls heard the sound of silvery laughter above their heads. When they looked up, they saw Zoe the Skating Fairy zip out of the tree. She flew down and hovered in the air in front of them! The girls had already met Zoe, and all the other Sports Fairies, when they'd first started their adventure. They were delighted to see her again. Zoe had long red hair, and wore a sporty

tank and leggings. A pretty blue pendant hung around her neck, sparkling in the sunshine.

"Did someone say they'd like some fairy wings?" she asked, smiling and twirling her wand between her fingers. "I can help with that."

"Oh, thank you," Rachel said eagerly. "We spotted four goblins on skates, Zoe, and we're sure they have your magic lace. They're skating incredibly well!"

"Unlike everyone else here today," Kirsty added, as a girl on rollerskates veered off the path nearby, barely missing a large bush.

Zoe winced as the girl fell face-first onto the grass. Luckily, she was wearing a helmet and wasn't hurt.

"Oops!" Zoe said. "I see what you mean, girls. Come behind this tree so you're out of sight, and I'll turn you into fairies."

Kirsty and Rachel did as she asked, and Zoe waved her wand over them.

Immediately, a shower of sparkling fairy dust surrounded the girls and transformed them into tiny fairies! Rachel fluttered

her wings in delight. "Come on!"
she cried. "Let's catch up
with those goblins."

"Fly high," Zoe
reminded the girls.
"We don't
want anyone
in the park
to spot us."

The three fairies
sped through
the air until they
saw the goblins
down below.

"They're lining up,"
Kirsty noticed. "What
are they doing?"

Rachel stared. The goblins
had split up, so that each one

was the same distance
away from the next.
"Is it some kind
of trap?" she
wondered nervously.
The friends
watched as the
goblin at the back
of the line began
skating along the
path toward his
friend. "He's got
my magic lace!" Zoe
exclaimed, pointing
at a glittering
object in his hand.
"What's he doing with it?"
As the goblin reached
his friend, he handed the

lace to him. Then the second goblin
skated off, while the first goblin stopped
and watched him go.

"They're practicing for a relay race,"
Kirsty realized.

"And they're using the magic lace as
a baton!" Rachel added.

Up ahead, the fairies could see that
a third goblin was
waiting in position,
near a cluster of
oak trees. Seeing
the oak trees gave
Rachel an idea.

"Zoe, I know it's
not the right season
for acorns, but do you think you might
be able to use your magic to put some
into those trees?"

"I sure can," Zoe replied, "but why?"

"If we can get to the trees before the
third goblin starts his part of the race,"
Rachel explained, "we can shower him
with magic acorns. Then, while he's
distracted, we could swoop down and
grab the lace!"

"That's a great idea!" Kirsty cried.
"We'd better hurry, though. The second
goblin will be ready to hand off the lace
soon."

The three fairies sped along as fast as
they could. Zoe pointed her wand at
the trees, and Rachel and Kirsty smiled

as they saw hundreds of sparkling fairy acorns appear among the leaves.

Meanwhile, down below, the second goblin had handed off the lace. The third goblin immediately set off on his skates through the trees, clutching the magic lace. As he did, Zoe waved her wand again and the tree branches began to shake. Soon, lots and lots of glittering green acorns showered down all around him.

Kirsty's Sweet Idea

"Help!" yelled the goblin, covering his head with his hands. "What's happening?"

"There's the lace!" Zoe exclaimed, spotting it between his fingers. "If I use my magic to keep the branches still, will you two try to get it?"

"Of course," Kirsty replied eagerly.

Zoe touched her wand to the branch

in front of her, and all the trees stopped
showering acorns. Kirsty and Rachel
immediately swooped down toward the
goblin's hand.

Unfortunately, now that the acorns had
stopped falling, the goblin had uncovered
his head and was staring up at the tree.
He soon noticed Kirsty and Rachel
speeding toward him!

"Where did you come from?" he cried, trying to skate away from them.

But there were so many acorns on the ground that the wheels of one skate jammed and the goblin lost his balance. His arms flailed, and the sparkling lace fell from his grip and dropped to the ground.

Rachel's eyes lit up as she saw it fall, and she lunged for it. Her fingers were just about to fold around the magic lace when the goblin thundered to the ground—and landed right on the lace.

Rachel and Kirsty were barely able
to dart out of the way in time to avoid
being squished. They looked at the goblin,
and then at each other. There was no
way they could get the magic lace now
that the goblin was sitting on it!

The goblin picked himself up and
grabbed the lace once again. Then he
stuck his tongue out at the fairies. "Keep

your sparkly acorns to yourself!" he snapped. "You're not getting the magic lace, and that's that!" Picking his way carefully through the acorns, he skated off toward the fourth goblin, farther down the path.

Zoe put her hands on her hips. "Oh, we almost had it!" She sighed. "Well, we'll just have to make a new plan."

Rachel and Kirsty nodded and, together, the three friends flew after the goblin. When they caught up, they could see that the relay was over, and the four goblins were now shouting at one another. The friends perched on a branch to listen.

"If you can't go faster than that, we'll drop you from the team!" the first goblin said, scolding the third.

"If you skate like that in the Fairyland Olympics, we'll lose," the second goblin added. "Jack Frost will be furious!"

"It wasn't my fault," the third goblin argued. "I was attacked!"

"Attacked?" laughed the fourth goblin. "By what?"

"By . . . an army!" the third goblin declared. "An army of fairies. They bombarded me with magic acorns!"

"Tiny little acorns?" the first goblin sneered. "So what?"

"No, no," the third goblin protested. "Not tiny little acorns. Enormous acorns. Acorns the size of soccer balls!"

Kirsty and Rachel tried not to laugh out loud as the goblin's story became less believable by the minute.

"They came at me from all angles," he

went on dramatically. "I could have been squished at any moment!"

The other goblins were wide-eyed. "Oh no, not squished!" the second one repeated, glancing around nervously.

The third goblin nodded. "I was lucky to escape alive," he boasted. "I had to fight heroically to save the magic lace."

"Good work," the first goblin said, clapping him on the back. "How did you keep it safe?"

The third goblin hesitated. "Um . . ." he began.

Rachel, Kirsty, and Zoe smiled at one another. He didn't want to admit that he'd kept the lace safe by sitting on it!

"I . . . I was just able to keep it out of their way," he replied at last.

Just then, a voice shouted from across the park, "Doughnuts! Come and get your yummy doughnuts! Free samples! Try before you buy!"

The girls looked around to see a man setting up a doughnut stand nearby. The goblins saw it, too.

"Oooh, doughnuts," the fourth goblin said, licking his lips. "I'm hungry!"

The first goblin shook his head. "We don't have time for doughnuts," he said seriously. "We need to keep practicing.

And we're supposed to be eating healthy food before the Olympics, not junk!" He ignored the fourth goblin's dismayed look and began giving orders. "So, we'll do the same practice run again, ending at this tree, OK?" He pointed to a large oak by the side of the path. "Like before, come back here for a time-check as soon as you've completed your part of the race. Now, everyone get in position!"

With a last longing look at the doughnut stall, the fourth goblin

trudged back to his position. So did
the others.

Kirsty looked thoughtfully at the
hungry goblin. *Just how much does he want a
doughnut?* she wondered. *Enough to fall for
a trick?*

Trick or Treat?

"I've got an idea," Kirsty whispered
to her friends. "Zoe, do you think that
you could make me look like a goblin?"

Zoe looked at Kirsty thoughtfully.
"I think so," she replied. "I'd just have
to turn your clothes into a tracksuit,
make you the right height, and tint
your skin green." She wrinkled her nose.

"But if the goblins look closely at you, they'll be able to see you're not a real goblin."

"If my plan works, that won't matter," Kirsty replied.

"What *is* your plan?" Rachel asked curiously.

"Well, we need to get that hungry goblin to leave his spot on the race track. Then I'll take his place," Kirsty explained. "When the third goblin skates up and hands over the magic lace, I'll skate away with it!"

"That's a great idea!" Zoe cried. "And the lace's powers will mean you can zoom off extra fast!" she added.

"But how will we persuade the goblin to leave the track?" Rachel asked.

The doughnut man began shouting

again, and Kirsty grinned.

"If you had a doughnut, Rachel, you could tempt the goblin with it. Then he might go to the doughnut seller and get one for himself," she said. "That way, Zoe will make me look like a goblin, and I'll stand in his place, ready to get the lace."

Zoe beamed. "One doughnut coming up!" she cried, waving her wand. With a fizz of fairy dust, Rachel grew to her usual size, and a warm, frosted doughnut appeared in midair. It hovered there for a moment, then drifted into Rachel's hand.

"Ooh, pleased to eat you," Rachel

said with a giggle. The doughnut
smelled delicious. Then she winked at
her friends. "Here I go!"

Rachel carefully climbed down the tree
and skated toward the goblin. She waved
the doughnut so that its yummy scent
drifted under his nose. Then she took a
bite. "*Mmm-mmm!*" she said loudly.

The goblin stared at
her and licked his lips.

"This is *soooo*
delicious," Rachel said,
taking another nibble.

The goblin glared at
her. "Go away!" he snapped. "I'm trying
to concentrate on the relay, and you're
distracting me."

"Sorry," Rachel said innocently. "It's
just that this doughnut is scrumptious."

The goblin watched her take another
bite, then a sly look crossed his face.
Suddenly, he reached out an arm and
grabbed at the doughnut. Rachel darted
out of the way.

"Give me that!" the goblin ordered
greedily.

"Get one for yourself," Rachel replied.

"The man over there is giving out free samples."

The goblin glanced over his shoulder longingly, but then he frowned. "It will be my turn to race soon," he said. "I'd better not."

"Oh, you've got plenty of time," Rachel told him. "Better not wait too long, though. The doughnut man may not have very many left . . ."

The goblin looked panicked at the  thought of missing out on a sweet treat! With one last look at Rachel's delicious doughnut, he quickly skated off. Rachel looked

up at Kirsty and Zoe as they flew down
to the ground. She was ready to put their
plan into action!

"It's goblin time for you!" Zoe said
to Kirsty, waving her wand.

Kirsty Races Into Trouble

Sparkly red fairy dust whirled around
fairy-sized Kirsty. She tingled all over,
then felt herself getting bigger and
bigger. Soon she was about half her
human size. When she looked down, she
saw that she was wearing a tracksuit
and her hands had turned green.

"Wow!" Rachel said. "You really could
pass for a goblin."

"But she's not as sneaky as a real one,"
Zoe added.

"I'll go and wait in the fourth goblin's
place on the track," Kirsty said.

"OK," Zoe replied. "We'll meet you by
the oak tree that marks the finish line.
Good luck!"

Kirsty stepped onto the path and
looked over her shoulder to see where

the third goblin in the relay was. He was
skating right toward her, so she whipped
her head back around again. She didn't
want him to get a good look at her face.
Her heart pounded with excitement. She
hoped her plan was
going to work!

She could hear the
third goblin's skates
as he came closer, so
Kirsty slowly began
skating. She stretched
her hand out behind
her, so she was ready
to take the lace.
Then, just as she
felt the third goblin
putting the magic
lace into her palm, she

heard an annoyed voice cry, "Hey! It's my turn!"

Kirsty turned and saw that the fourth goblin was back. He was munching his doughnut and looked surprised to see her in his place. Kirsty could only think of one thing to do—she grabbed the lace from the third goblin and took off at top speed before either of the goblins could catch her!

"What's going on?" she heard the fourth goblin yell as she sped away.

Meanwhile, Zoe had transformed Rachel back into a fairy. The two fairies had flown to the finish line, and watched everything from above. They saw the third and fourth goblins stare at each other, and then at Kirsty, who was now skating away. Then the fairies saw the goblins suddenly realize that Kirsty wasn't a goblin at all!

"We've been tricked!" the goblin with the doughnut shouted furiously. "It was all your fault, giving her the magic lace like that! Couldn't you tell it wasn't me?"

"It wasn't my fault!" the third goblin retorted. "If you had stayed in your position like you were supposed to, none of this would have happened!"

"Well, we need to catch her," the goblin with the doughnut said. "Right now!"

The two goblins began skating after Kirsty. Now that they no longer had the magic lace, they couldn't go as fast as before, but they kept skating, puffing and panting as they went.

Rachel noticed that the two goblins

who had skated the first part of the
relay had doubled back. They were now
heading toward the finish line, too, but
from the opposite direction. One of them
nudged the other and pointed ahead at
Kirsty, who was racing toward them.

"Oh no!" Rachel cried. "The other

two goblins have spotted Kirsty!"

Rachel and Zoe immediately headed
toward Kirsty, too. The two goblins who
had been early in the relay seemed to
have realized something was wrong,
because they suddenly started skating
much faster.

"They're going to try to head her off!" Zoe realized.

"Poor Kirsty," Rachel cried in horror. "She'll be caught in the middle of all four goblins!"

Rachel and Zoe flew toward Kirsty as fast as they could.

"I'll turn Kirsty into a fairy," Zoe decided. "Then she can fly up into the air, away from the goblins."

"What about the magic lace?" Rachel reminded her. "It might be too heavy for her to carry when she's a fairy."

Zoe shook her head. "Don't worry," she said. "The magic objects change size according to who's holding 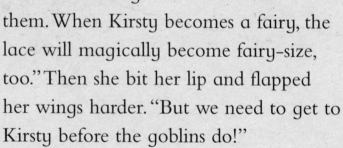 them. When Kirsty becomes a fairy, the lace will magically become fairy-size, too." Then she bit her lip and flapped her wings harder. "But we need to get to Kirsty before the goblins do!"

Rachel nodded. They had to get to Kirsty in time . . . otherwise her friend would be trapped by four goblins!

Rachel and Zoe couldn't let that happen!

Flying High

Down on the path, Kirsty glanced over her shoulder to see that the two goblins were still behind her, glaring as they gave chase. But when she turned her head and looked forward again, she gasped in shock. Skating straight toward her were the first and second goblins!

Kirsty looked all around, but there was
no way out. She couldn't skate off the
path and onto the grass, because there
was a tennis court fence on one side
and flowerbeds on the other. She was
trapped!

The goblins were closing in, and
Kirsty felt sick with fright. They were
so close now that she could hear them
shouting at her to give back the skating
lace.

The goblins stretched out their arms, reaching for the magic lace.

"Help!" Kirsty cried, wondering where Zoe and Rachel were, and hoping they would hear her. "Help!"

And then, at the very last second, just as one of the goblins was about to snatch the magic lace, she saw a cloud of bright sparkles swirl around her, and felt herself shrinking down, down, down . . .

It was such a relief to feel wings on her
back and find
that she was a fairy
again! Kirsty zipped
up into the air,
flapping her wings
as hard as she
could. The goblins
below jumped up
and down, trying to
grab a hold of her.

"Kirsty, are you OK?" Rachel cried, as
she and Zoe flew over to her. They were
out of breath, too!

"Yes," Kirsty replied faintly. "That was
close, though. Thanks, Zoe!"

The three fairies landed on the branch
of a nearby oak tree to catch their breath.
Instantly, the goblins tried to climb the

tree. They still had their skates on, though, so it was a struggle.

Zoe put her hands on her hips and shouted down to them. "Any more trouble from the four of you, and I really *will* make magic acorns the size of soccer balls drop on you!" she warned. "Then you'll be goblin pancakes!"

The goblins hesitated. "I don't want to be a goblin pancake!" wailed one, sliding down the tree trunk.

"Me neither," the others said in chorus as they stumbled away from the oak. Soon, the four goblins were skating away as fast as they could.

Kirsty handed Zoe the magic lace, smiling.

Zoe looked delighted to have it back.
"Thank you
so much!"
she exclaimed.
She touched
her wand
to the lace,
and a flash
of bright
red sparkles
surrounded it.
"There," she said
happily. "Now
everything will be back to normal with
skaters everywhere."

The three fairies flew down to the
ground. Zoe waved her wand over
Kirsty and Rachel, magically turning
them back to their normal size.

"Thanks again, girls," she said. "Enjoy
the rest of your time in the park. You'll
find skating much more fun now, I
promise."

"Thanks, Zoe," Rachel replied. "It was
great helping you. Good-bye!"

"Good-bye," Kirsty added.

"Bye, girls," Zoe said. With a burst
of red fairy dust that sparkled in the

air for a second, she was gone.

Rachel nudged Kirsty as a group of boys went by on in-line skates, whooping as they pulled off some tricky-looking turns. "Look, everyone's skating well again," she said.

Rachel was right. Nobody was falling over anymore. All the skaters and skateboarders looked like they were having a great time as they sped along.

Kirsty grinned. "I bet we'll be able to skate better now, too," she said happily. "Come on, let's find out. I'll race you to that tree!"

The two friends skated off together,

laughing as they went. Another magic object was safely back with its fairy keeper—now there were just four left to find. And Rachel and Kirsty were just the girls to find them!

THE SPORTS FAIRIES

Rachel and Kirsty now need to help

Brittany

the Basketball Fairy!

The pesky goblins stole the magic
basketball, and Brittany is determined
to get it back! Can Rachel and Kirsty help
make basketball fun for everyone again?

Join their next adventure in
this special sneak peek!

Spring into Sports

"What should we do after lunch, Kirsty?"
Rachel Walker asked as she finished
her apple.

Kirsty Tate, Rachel's best friend, grinned.
"You know what I'd really like to do?"
she replied. "I'd like to find Brittany the
Basketball Fairy's magic basketball!"

"Remember what Queen Titania told us,"
Rachel reminded Kirsty. "We have to
let the magic come to us."

"I know, but I'm feeling really impatient today," Kirsty replied. "If we don't find all the magic objects before I go home in a few days, Jack Frost and his goblins will win the Fairyland Olympics Cup!"

Rachel sighed. "The missing objects mean that sports in our world are affected too," she added. "I wonder how many basketball games are going wrong right now because Brittany's basketball is missing!"

Rachel nodded. "We can't let Jack Frost and his goblins win the cup by cheating," she said seriously. "Especially since King Oberon told us that the cup is filled with good luck. Imagine all the mischief the goblins could cause with lots of luck to help them!"

RAINBOW magic

These activities are magical!
Play dress-up, send friendship notes, and much more!

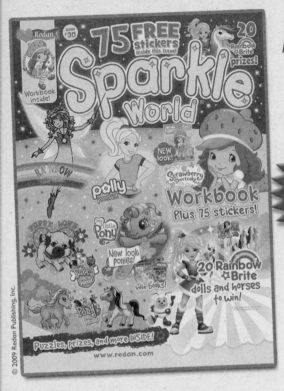

RAINBOW magic™

There's Magic in Every Series!

The Rainbow Fairies

The Weather Fairies

The Jewel Fairies

The Pet Fairies

The Fun Day Fairies

The Petal Fairies

The Dance Fairies

The Music Fairies

The Sports Fairies

The Party Fairies

Read them all!

📖 SCHOLASTIC

www.scholastic.com

www.rainbowmagiconline.com

HIT entertainment

RMFAIRY2